Artic

N

W · E

S

Xian, China

COTLAND (N Y) FREE LIBRARY

A

Darjeeling, India

chartered 1925

Thailand

Nile Valley, Egypt

Kenya

DISCARD

Darwin, Australia

Antartica

To those intrepid weather watchers,
Debbie and Jerry Aronson

—M.S.

For Aunt Carol

—F.L.

Many thanks to all the folks who helped lift the fog: Steve Aronson,

Renée Cafiero, Anne Calmette-Fosse, Betty Conley, Leni Friedman, Frank Hess, Simone Kaplan,

Ann Kent, Jack Kent, Jay Kerig, Frané Lessac, Donn Livingston, David Lubar, Zubin Medora,

John Pollack, Dian Curtis Regan, Matt Rosen, James Rozak, Amy Edgar Sklansky, Roland Smith,

Patrick J. Tyson, Phoebe Yeh, and everyone at HarperCollins.

On the Same Day in March
A Tour of the World's Weather
Text copyright © 2000 by Marilyn Singer
Illustrations copyright © 2000 by Frané Lessac
Printed in the U.S.A. All rights reserved.
http://www.harperchildrens.com

Library of Congress Cataloging-in-Publication Data
Singer, Marilyn.
    On the same day in March : a tour of the world's weather / Marilyn Singer ;
illustrated by Frané Lessac.
        p.   cm.
    Summary: Highlights a wide variety of weather conditions by taking a tour around
the world and examining weather in different places on the same day in March.
    ISBN 0-06-028187-1. — ISBN 0-06-028188-X (lib. bdg.)
    1. Climatology—Juvenile literature.   2. Weather—Juvenile literature.
[1. Weather.]   I. Lessac, Frané, ill.   II. Title.
QC981.3.S57   2000   98-52797
551.6—dc21   CIP
                                                                                AC

Typography by Michele N. Tupper
1   2   3   4   5   6   7   8   9   10
❖
First Edition

On the Same Day in March
A Tour of the World's Weather

Marilyn Singer

illustrated by Frané Lessac

HARPERCOLLINSPUBLISHERS

In the **Arctic**

Polar bears ride on floes of ice,
stalking seals,
wishing fish,
as the six-month sun begins to rise
slowly in the Arctic skies.

On the same day in March . . .

in **Alberta, Canada**

Just when you can't even remember spring,
that wild chinook blows in like a dragon,
and quicker than you can say Medicine Hat,
the biggest snow fort ever
is nothing but a dragon-shaped patch
in somebody's backyard.

On the same day in March . . .

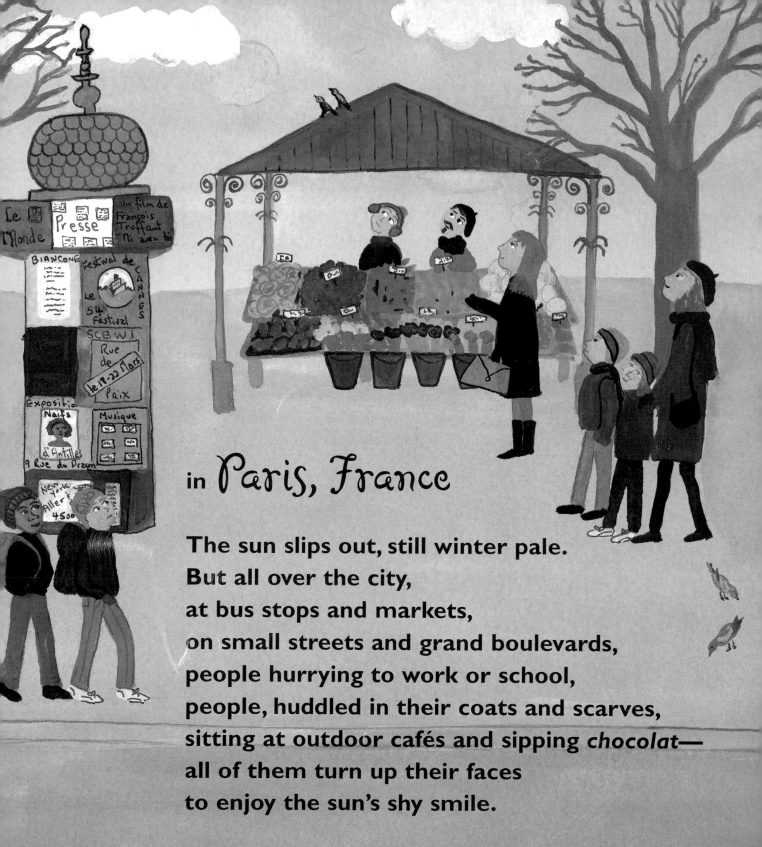

in *Paris, France*

The sun slips out, still winter pale.
But all over the city,
at bus stops and markets,
on small streets and grand boulevards,
people hurrying to work or school,
people, huddled in their coats and scarves,
sitting at outdoor cafés and sipping *chocolat*—
all of them turn up their faces
to enjoy the sun's shy smile.

On the same day in March . . .

in **New York City**

It's too gray to play outside today.
The parents sigh, the little kids complain.
But the basketball players stay in the school yard,
arguing what's worse—
snow or sleet or freezing rain.

On the same day in March . . .

in the Texas Panhandle

They said it was just a tiny twister—
not big enough to spin a horse
or hoist a cow.
But it did suck up a bucket of water
and give Grandma's dirty old truck
the first wash it's had in weeks.

On the same day in March . . .

in the *Nile Valley*

Fog threads through the temples.

in a **Louisiana bayou**

Fog settles on the swamp.

On the same day in March . . .

in Xian, China

In the park
the old men and small children guess:
What will the wind carry today?
Clouds of blue-winged swallows,
dust that hurts their eyes,
rain from up the mountain,
kites shaped like butterflies?

On the same day in March . . .

in Darjeeling, India

Hailstones all over the hillside!
No one is happy
except little sister,
who thinks the moon has broken and scattered
its necklace of pearls.

On the same day in March . . .

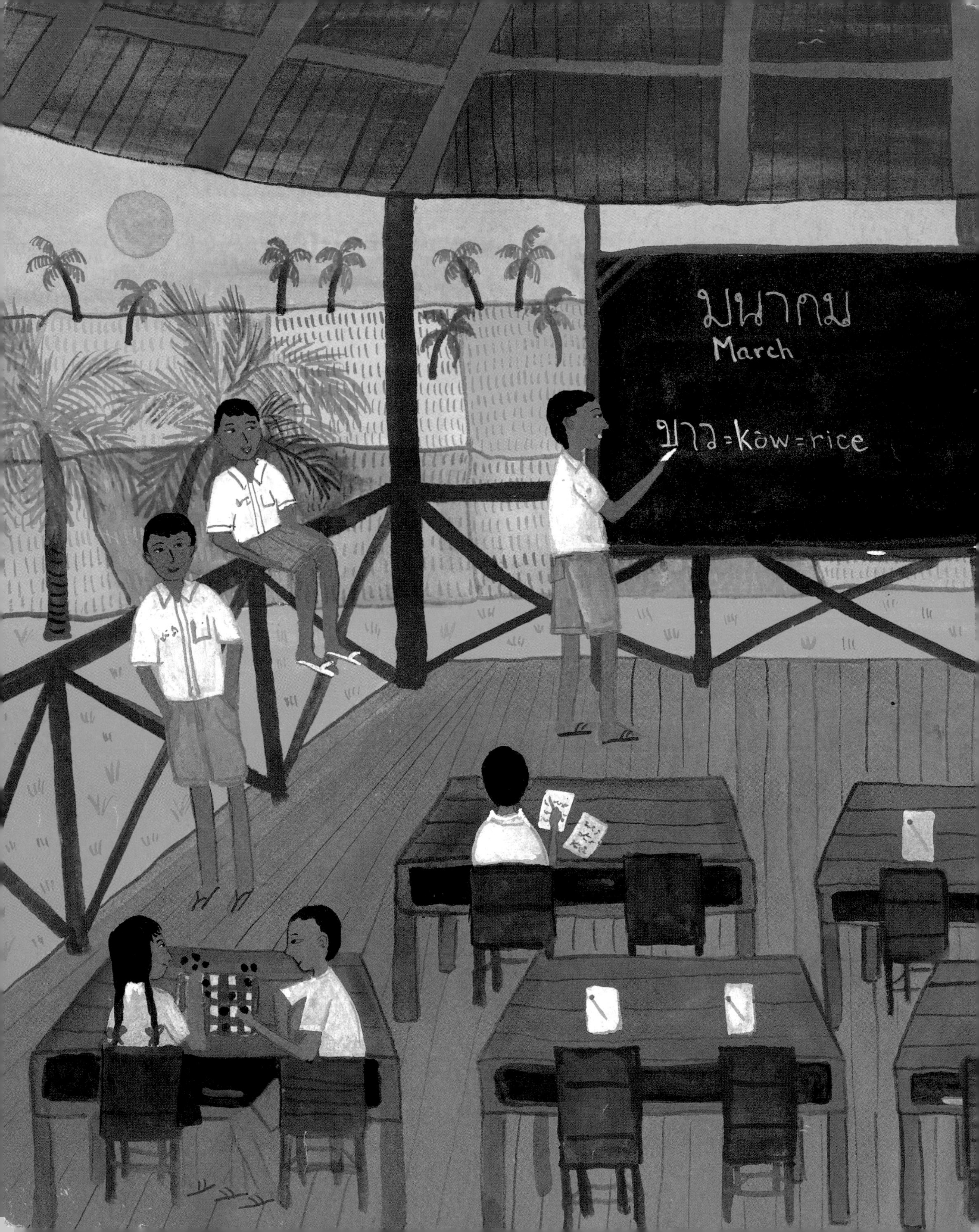
มนาคม
March
ขาว = kôw = rice

RICE

in *Central Thailand*

It's too hot to plant rice.
It's too hot to pick rice.
But it's not too hot to *spell* R I C E
on the blackboard in the school.

On the same day in March . . .

in Dakar, Senegal
Sunlight sparkles on the market.

in **Barbados**

Sunlight dazzles on the sand.

On the same day in March . . .

The rains come,
and all in one day,
they leave the gift of a river.
Everyone, hurry!
Come drink! Come play!
Before the sun shines
and, all in one day,
takes the river away.

On the same day in March . . .

in the **Amazon Basin, Brazil**

Grandpapa is always late.
The rain is always on time,
arriving at three o'clock yesterday,
three o'clock tomorrow,
three o'clock today.
"Only the weather wears a watch,"
Grandpapa likes to say,
whenever he or the rain makes everyone wait.

On the same day in March . . .

in Darwin, Australia

Board up the windows!
Bring in the boat!
Better to be like crocodiles crouched on the shore
than to be out sailing the sea
when the willy-willies come to call.

On the same day in March . . .

in Patagonia, Argentina

Over the wide, dry plain
autumn shears the clouds like a flock of sheep.
"Catch the wool," Mama teases her youngest son.
He doesn't understand why these white puffs
vanish wet and cold
in his fat warm hands.

On the same day in March . . .

in Antarctica

Penguins scramble on the shore,
seeking mates,
missing fish,
as the six-month sun begins to slice
down below the Antarctic ice.

All on the same day in March!

A Note from the Author

It takes the earth 365 days—one year—to make a complete trip around the sun. The earth does not sit straight up and down in the heavens. It tilts on its axis— an imaginary line running through the center. The top of the axis is the North Pole; the bottom is the South Pole. As the earth orbits, sometimes the North Pole tips toward the sun, and sometimes it tips away from the sun. This tilt is what gives us the seasons.

In March, winter turns to spring in the Northern Hemisphere, and summer turns to fall in the Southern Hemisphere. The North Pole will soon lean closer to the sun, giving the Arctic six months of daylight and warmer weather. The South Pole will lean farther and farther away from the sun, slipping Antarctica into six months of darkness and bitter cold. On any given day in March, somewhere in the world, it may be raining, snowing, or hailing. It may be sunny, foggy, or windy.

There are places where the weather doesn't change much throughout the year. For example, in the equatorial rain forests, it is hot and humid and it does rain at the same time every day. There are other parts of the world where the weather can sometimes change from hour to hour. New York City, where I live, is one of those places.

Marilyn Singer

MARCH

			1	2	3	4
5	6	7	8	9	10	11
12	13	14	15	16	17	18
19	20	21	22	23	24	25
26	27	28	29	30	31	

Alberta, Canada

New York City, U.S.A.

Paris, France

Louisiana Bayou, U.S.A.

Texas Panhandle, U.S.A.

Barbados

Dakar, Senegal

Amazon Basin, Brazil

Patagonia, Argentina